Veronica Twitch

DOUBLE-BUBBLE
girl band trouble!

Erica-Jane Waters

WACKY B

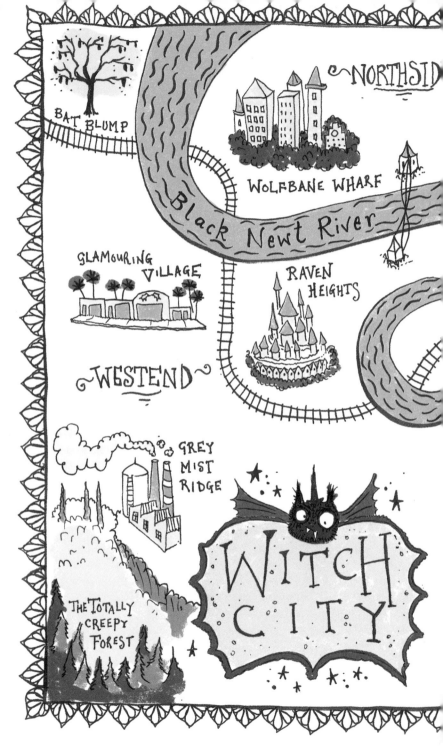

VERONICA

Name: Veronica

Job Title: Editor-in-Chief, *Twitch* magazine

Loves: Stationery

Can't live without: Chocolate Battachinos

Familiar: Pop the Chihuahua

What's in her hand-cauldron?:
Pens (all colours), highlighters (all colours), phone, keys, galaxy notes, hair brush

Name: Figgy

Job Title: Stylist at *Twitch* magazine

Loves: Pom-poms

Can't live without: Her sewing kit

Familiar: Sparkle the Chihuahua

What's in her hand-cauldron?:

Needle & thread, tape measure,
lip balm, emergency false eyelashes

BUTTONS

STYLE
V.I.W INVITE
FRONT ROW
WITCH CITY FASHION WEEK

Fashion C
INVITE

FRONT ROW

BROOM TUBE

Name: Pru

Job Title: Photographer, *Twitch* magazine

Loves: Organising

Can't live without: Her laminator

Familiar: Puff the Chihuahua

What's in her hand-cauldron?:
Broom-Tube map, hair bobbles, organiser, handwipes, spare everything

PUMPKIN
LIP BALM

Chapter One
Three at the Cauldron Café

"Three Cherry Charm Sparkle Smoothies, please, with extra cherries. We've got a lot to discuss!"

Veronica popped her purse back in her hand-cauldron and carried the tray of drinks over to the velvet-covered sofa where her friends and work buddies at *Twitch* magazine, Figgy and

Pru, were sitting (along with Pop, Sparkle and Puff, the witches' Chihuahua familiars). The Cauldron Café was the cosiest place in Witch City in which to meet friends, with cool music and delicious drinks and cakes.

"So what's the assignment this week, Veronica? I just bought a new lens for my camera and I can't wait to use it." Pru lifted her camera to her eye and pretended to snap photos of her friends.

"And there's a fabulous new fashion store that's just opened in Raven Heights," Figgy told them, moving Puff off her lap and onto the chair next to Pop and Sparkle, "full of really fun stuff – perfect for styling our next feature."

Veronica took a slurp of her cherry smoothie and jiggled about excitedly on her seat. "Well, it's funny you should mention Raven Heights because that's exactly where we're headed straight after this." Pop barked with excitement.

Figgy and Pru both leaned in closer, eager to hear who or what was going to be *Twitch* magazine's next big story. As editor and star interviewer, Veronica was always coming up with exciting new ideas.

"Has either of you ever heard of a little band called… oh, what's their name again?"

Veronica took another slurp of her drink, enjoying teasing her friends.

"Is it who I think it is? Is it? Oh, my stars, is it really?" Figgy was so excited she didn't notice she had dribbled cherry smoothie all down her chin and dress.

"It might be," Veronica said as she patted her friend's outfit with a napkin, but only managed to make the stain bigger.

TODAY'S
SPECIAL

Spiced Pumpkin
Hot Chocolate
with Blackberry
Syrup

"So it's a band, and it's a band from Raven Heights, and they must be big because I've actually never seen you acting so silly," said Pru, moving everybody's hand-cauldrons away from Figgy's cherry smoothie, to avert any sticky-drink-related accessories disaster.

"It's Double-Bubble! It is, isn't it!" Figgy jumped up off the sofa before being swiftly dragged back down by Veronica.

"Yes," she said in a hushed tone, "it is Double-Bubble. They're performing a surprise concert at Witchfest this weekend. It will be their biggest gig to date and we get back-stage passes and access all areas with the band!

"But we don't want half the Cauldron Café and Witch City getting wind of this – it's our exclusive and we need to keep it under our witchy hats! Imagine if *Nosy Toad* magazine

got a whiff of this and tried to steal the story…
it would look very unprofessional, and Double-
Bubble might even drop out of the interviews
and photo shoots, or, worse still, decide to let
Nosy Toad cover their big gig instead!"

"Did I hear my magazine mentioned?" asked
a voice from behind the girls.

"Urgh, it's Belinda Bullfrog, where did she come
from!" Pru muttered under her breath while
she and the others tried to smile innocently.

Belinda Bullfrog was Editor-in-Chief of *Nosy
Toad*, *Twitch* magazine's greatest rival. The
two publications were very different, though.
Belinda Bullfrog and her team seemed more
interested in selling as many copies of their
magazine as they could and making lots
of money, rather than celebrating positive
news and promoting inspirational witches
as Veronica preferred to do.

"Having a little meeting, are we?" Belinda said, looking down her nose at the three young witches. "Maybe you should take some hints and tips from my magazine. After all, we are the biggest and best publication in Witch City."

Pop, Sparkle and Puff growled at Belinda as she pulled a copy of *Nosy Toad* out of her hand-cauldron and tossed it onto the table in front of them.

"Must catch up for lunchy-poos soon, ladies," she snorted, and with that turned on her heel and left the café.

The three friends glanced at each other nervously.

"How much did she hear?" Figgy whispered, her voice shaking a little.

"I don't know, but we shouldn't talk any more about it in here. It's too public," said Veronica firmly. "Let's grab our things and get going. It's a long Broom-Tube ride to Raven Heights and we don't want to be late for our meeting with you-know-who."

The three witches finished their cherry smoothies, grabbed their hand-cauldrons and Chihuahua familiars and made their way out of the café into the hustle and bustle of Witch City and on to Grand Central Broom Station.

Chapter Two

A Broom-Tube Ride to Raven Heights

At Grand Central Broom Station a chilly wind whooshed behind them as the three witches took the escalator down to the underground Broom-Tube. Veronica shivered a little and rubbed her arms as they jostled through the crowded underground passageways to try and find the right platform for Raven Heights.

20

"The underground Broom-Tube is so confusing, we'll never find the right place. There are 320 platforms! And why is it always so cold down here?" she wailed.

"If you chose practical clothes instead of fashionable ones, you might not be so cold," sniped Pru, pulling her sensible felt hat down over her ears and looking a tad annoyed by her friend's behaviour.

Veronica rolled her eyes. "I'm the one who's suffering here!" she retorted. "Why are you getting all witch-snippety with me?"

Figgy pulled her friends to one side. "Listen, you two," she said in a soothing voice, "we always get a bit stressed when we have to go on the Broom-Tube. It's busy and loud and confusing. Let's not argue as well, okay?"

Veronica and Pru looked at each other for a moment and then burst into giggles.

Their peacemaker friend always knew how to deal with squabbles and bring everyone back together.

"Sorry, Veronica," said Pru, pulling a little woollen cape out of her oversized hand-cauldron. "Have this, it'll help keep you warm."

"Thanks, Pru," she replied, "and as you are always so sensible, I don't suppose you brought a Broom-Tube map, did you?"

Pru rummaged in her cloak pocket before handing Veronica a perfectly laminated, folding Broom-Tube map with a red circle around Raven Heights station and a blue one around the platform they needed to take: number 9, southbound.

"I knew we could count on you!" Veronica told her. "There's platform 9, right ahead of us."

The long Broom-Tube pulled up to the platform and Veronica, Pru and Figgy jostled to get a seat, holding Pop, Sparkle and Puff on their laps. The three witches held on tight as the Broom set off through the dark tunnels on its way to Raven Heights.

Veronica looked around her at the other witches on the Broom-Tube. Some were reading the newspaper; some were listening to music on their headphones. There was a group of little school witches all giggling excitedly and an old married witch couple, with a tiny black cat sitting in between them.

"This is it," said Pru, "Raven Heights Station. We're here!"

The Broom-Tube came to a sudden stop, causing everyone to sway a little in their seats. The girls dismounted and joined the throng of witches elbowing their way towards the escalators and up to the street above.

Raven Heights was right in the middle of Witch City but felt more like a little hilltop town. The cobbled streets twisted and turned, up and up and up, climbing past dimly lit coffee shops, record stores playing mysterious music and lots of very cool and kooky-looking clothes shops. There were buskers playing instruments on the cobbles, their upturned witches' hats full of coins.

"My feet hurt," Veronica muttered, before remembering it probably wasn't a good idea to complain since she had chosen to wear her smartest extra-pointy shoes today.

"It certainly is a steep climb to the top of Raven Heights," sighed Pru, perusing a map of the area that she had also laminated.

"The Belfry Bistro is right at the top of the hill, on the corner of Black Newt View," said Figgy.

Veronica and Pru both glanced at their friend, astonished by her apparent knowledge of the area.

"What? Can't I be the organised one for once?" she laughed.

The girls pushed on up the final few streets before reaching the top of Raven Heights.

"Wow, what a view!" said Figgy as they looked around.

The midday sun was shining down on the Black Newt river as it twisted through Witch City below.

"Look, I can see our office from here," said Veronica, pointing to the faint silhouette of Wolfbane Wharf in the misty distance.

Just then the Belfry Tower bell chimed twelve.

"Come on, ladies," said Veronica, "we've got an exclusive interview to get to!"

Veronica, Pru and Figgy clip-clopped
their way over the cobbles and
in through the dark doorway
of the Belfry Bistro.

Chapter Three

V.I.W.
(Very Important Witch)

Veronica and her friends were greeted at
the door by one of the Belfry Bistro's snooty
waiting staff.

"Table for three?" she said, her black-painted
lips barely moving as she spoke.

"Actually, we're here to meet someone.
We have a reservation," Veronica replied
with a twinkle in her eye.

"Name?" the witch said with a sigh as she ran a long, white finger down her reservations list.

"Twitch… Veronica Twitch."

The waitress witch's tone suddenly changed. "Oh, I see. Well, you need to come this way, to the V.I.W. area."

The three witches followed her as she shuffled ahead, unable to take a proper stride due to the tightness of her dress. She pulled back a heavy, black velvet curtain and ushered them through. Once inside, they were seated and handed a drinks menu.

"What's a 'Charred Sour Fizzy Slip'?"
Figgy asked Veronica.

"I don't know," she had to admit.

"And what's a 'Burned Aroma of Log Puff'?"

"I can't make head nor tail of this menu.
Don't they just do a nice cup of tea?" said Pru.
"In fact, I don't think we're cool enough to
be here…"

Just then there was a flurry of activity and
a dazzle of camera flashes as two veiled
figures made their way over to the table
where the girls were sitting.

"It's them," gulped Figgy. "It's Double-
Bubble."

"Just be calm," whispered Veronica, "we
don't want them thinking we're not cool."

"But I don't even understand the drinks menu," whimpered Pru.

"Oooh, I'm desperate for a cup of tea!" came a friendly voice from under one of the veils as Double-Bubble plonked themselves down at the table, their crow familiars perched on their shoulders. "I'm Jo, and this is my sister and bandmate Kit."

Now that the duo had pulled back their lacy veils it was clear they were normal witches, just like Veronica and her friends.

"What are you three drinking?" asked Kit.

"Erm, I... we were going have a..." stuttered Veronica.

"Oh, yes, I see." Jo winked at her. "The Belfry Bistro and its fancy drinks list that no one understands, though everyone's too cool to admit it!

"Pot of tea for five, please!" she shouted over to the witch waitress. "And a plate of your best choccy biccies!"

"Sounds perfect," said Veronica, happy to find Double-Bubble so down to earth and friendly. "We're just so excited that you've agreed to do this interview with *Twitch* magazine – we're going to have such fun! This is Figgy, our stylist, and Pru, our photographer."

"We can't wait to get started," said Jo. "What's the plan, then?"

"Well, Figgy here is going to scour the coolest boutiques in Raven Heights for some outfits and props for the shoot and for you to wear at the Witchfest concert. And Pru is going to scout for awesome locations where she'll shoot the photos. I'll be interviewing you, of course, and then writing the piece."

"And on that note," said Pru, looking at her watch, "I think we'd better get a move on; we've got a lot to do!"

Pru and Figgy said their goodbyes and left Veronica to talk to the famous sisters. After another pot of tea the interview was nearly wrapped up.

"Just one last question," said Veronica, chewing the end of her pen. "I'm curious about something. You both seem so laidback and calm despite the complete chaos that must come with being the number one band in Witch City... how do you cope with the pressure?"

"Good question," said Jo as she turned to her sister and blinked her long eyelashes three times. Kit blinked exaggeratedly back at her.

Veronica looked confused.

"It's okay," laughed Jo. "It's the secret system

33

we use to let each other know when we've had enough or need help and don't want to say so out loud. The press tends to take everything we say and twist it around."

"But *Twitch* never does that. We pride ourselves…"

"Oh, my stars, we know!" Kit interrupted her. "That's why we want you to have this exclusive. We love the way your magazine is so inspirational to young witches."

"Thank you," said Veronica, adjusting her pointy hat and smiling at the compliment. "Is there anything else you'd like to share before we wrap this up?"

"Well," said Jo, looking at her sister and receiving a nod in response, "there is one secret we'd like to share with you, but please don't print it in the article. We like you, Veronica, and trust you, so we'd like you to know."

"Of course you can trust me," she told them proudly.

"When the paparazzi shout questions at us in the street, like 'Who designed that dress?' or 'Where are you going?' we always say the complete opposite of what's true. It's a little game we like to play with them," Jo explained.

Veronica laughed. "I'll have to remember that, it must cause confusion!"

Double-Bubble stood up, re-veiled themselves and set their crows back on their shoulders.

"It's been lovely to meet you. Please send our warmest wishes to Figgy and Pru. We can't wait to meet again for the photo shoot and see this exclusive article all come together."

"The pleasure was all mine," replied Veronica as she watched the most famous girl band in Witch City sweep out of the back door.

Veronica picked up her familiar and made her way out of the Belfry Bistro.

"What's up, Pop?" she said sweetly to her Chihuahua, who was now barking madly and trying to wriggle out of her arms. "There's nothing there, you silly pooch."

But as she made her way down to the Broom-Tube to travel back to the magazine's office, she couldn't shake off the feeling that Pop had seen something she hadn't.

Chapter Four
A Crow-Napping

By the time Veronica had made it back to
Twitch HQ, it was late in the afternoon.
The large open-plan office was thronged
with witches wheeling rail after rail of stylish
clothes in every direction. There were stacks
of *Twitch* magazines piled up on shelves,
signed photos on the walls of all the famous
sports witches, actors and successful business
witches who had appeared in the magazine,
and important-looking meetings taking place
behind glass partitions.

Veronica plopped her heavy hand-cauldron down on her chair and started to empty out its contents. She pressed a button on her desk phone.

"Binky, could you bring me a frosted bataccino with extra cream, please? It's going to take me hours to write up this interview."

A minute later, her assistant appeared with the hot drink.

"Here you go, Veronica. What's up with Mr Cutie-Pie?" she asked, making a fuss of Pop.

"Thanks, Binky. I don't know what the matter is with him this afternoon. He's all fidgety and not himself at all."

"He's had a long day," said the girl as she watched Pop sigh and snuggle up in his basket under Veronica's desk. "Give me a buzz if you need anything else."

As Binky skipped away, Pru and Figgy swooshed in with a rail of clothes and a thick wad of photographs.

"Look at these boots!" Figgy crooned, wafting them under Veronica's nose as if they were a sweet, edible witchy treat.

TWITCH

"And look at this incredible location I found in Raven Heights for our photo shoot with Double-Bubble," said Pru. "Have you arranged a time with them for the shoot? We need to get that organised."

"Hold your unicorns!" Veronica said, handing back the cloak she had borrowed from Pru. "One thing at a time!"

"Sorry," said her friend, realising that her overly organised nature was not helping right now.

"No, you're right, I should call them straight away. Where is the location?"

Pru pointed to a place on another laminated map, while looking a bit embarrassed.

"What can I say? I like laminating things," she muttered.

Veronica and Figgy smiled at each other.

"We love you and your epic organisational

skills, Pru, and your equally epic stationery collection!"

Their laughter was interrupted by a sudden shriek from Binky.

"Veronica!" the girl squealed as she rushed over, clutching a laptop. "This email just came in for you from Belinda Bullfrog. Look."

From: belindabullfrog@nosytoad.com
To: veronicatwitch@twitch.com
Subject: Bad news, babes

Darling, looks like your big scoop with Double-Bubble is no more... switch on your TV.

Kissy-poos, Belinda

"Binky, grab the remote," Veronica said, turning towards the flat-screen TV on the office wall.

The young witches watched in horror at the news breaking in front of them.

Double-Bubble have been kidnapped and turned into crows...

BREAKING NEWS... GIRL BAND DOUBLE-BUBBLE HAVE BEEN CROW-NAPPED....

A horrified Veronica could not believe what she was hearing.

The girl band was last seen leaving the Belfry Bistro in Raven Heights shortly after 1pm this afternoon. This grainy video has been sent to WBC within the last hour and appears to show the band as crows…

Veronica squinted her eyes at the blurry image on the screen.

"Binky, can you rewind live TV?" she asked.

"Yes, sure," said her assistant, rewinding the blurred clip of two crows.

"Look… there!" gasped Veronica. "They're blinking at us, trying to communicate! Turn it up, Binky."

The witches listened to a series of harsh squawks.

"Anyone here speak Crow?" Figgy asked gloomily.

47

"No, but I can do a birdsong translation spell," Pru chipped in. "I had to learn it when I was working on *Twitch*'s Twitcher column last month."

"You need to put that spell on me," Veronica insisted. "Right now!"

She closed her eyes ready for Pru to cast her spell, while at the same time making a mental note to find out what exactly the Twitcher column was.

Pru emptied out her hand-cauldron and reached inside her hat, pulling out a small, blue bottle. She popped off the lid and emptied its contents into her cauldron. She plucked a feather off a boa that was hanging on a rail nearby and dropped it into the cauldron, along with a glass of water, a paper clip, two sticky notes and a highlighter pen.

Veronica opened one eye and saw the confused expressions on her friends' faces.

"Does anyone have anything bird-shaped?" asked Pru, finally.

"Here you go!" Figgy unfastened her raven-shaped necklace and passed it to her.

"Perfect!" Pru whispered a few words and squawks, walked around the cauldron three times, flapping her arms and bobbing her head back and forth, before there was a sudden flash and a wisp of starry purple smoke. It wafted over Veronica and spiralled into her ears.

"Okay," Pru exclaimed proudly, "you're good to go – I mean, squawk."

Binky replayed the video of Double-Bubble.

"Squawk, squawk… squawk, squawk."

Veronica cupped her hand to her ear. "Rain hats, rain hats… they're saying rain hats!"

"Rain hats? What sort of lame clue is that?" scoffed Pru.

"No, it's a brilliant one," Figgy said, happy that she had already solved it. "When I was shopping for outfits for Double-Bubble earlier in Raven Heights, there was one boutique that was selling rain hats. They are the latest craze and the shop was full of witches queuing up to buy them."

"Rain hats?" Pru repeated, struggling to understand the logic.

"Yes," Figgy continued, "they don't protect you from the rain, they rain on you, so you can fit right in with the gloomy set in Raven Heights, no matter what the weather."

"I've never heard anything so completely ridiculous in all my days," Pru complained.

"Well, ridiculous or not," said Veronica decisively, "we need to go to that shop and find Double-Bubble before we lose our exclusive interview. I just know Belinda Bullfrog and her seedy magazine are behind this. She must have overheard us in the Cauldron Café this morning – how else would she know about our big scoop?"

"Do you think Belinda kidnapped… I mean, crow-napped the band?" Figgy asked, looking fearful.

"I don't know," said Veronica as she slid her arm reassuringly around her friend. "But I do know that we'll find them soon and turn them back into a girl band! Come on, let's get back to that hat shop before it closes."

Veronica, Figgy and Pru grabbed their hand-cauldrons, kissed their sleeping familiars goodbye and swept out of the office in search of Double-Bubble.

Chapter Five
Rain Hats and Sticky Lippy

The shadows cast by the turreted buildings of Raven Heights were growing longer as the girls arrived there for the second time that day.

"Do you remember where the hat boutique is, Figgy?" asked Veronica

"Right at the very, very top!"

"Typical," Pru sighed as she huffed and puffed up the twisty, cobbled street. "No complaints about your sore feet this time, Veronica?"

She turned to smile at her friend only to find her floating along, her feet not even touching the ground.

"A levitation spell was the only way to solve my pointy-toe problems." She smiled smugly and flourished her wand at her pain-free feet.

"This is it!" Pru suddenly exclaimed, dashing over to a quaint little shopfront with dark blue-painted woodwork and a sign in the shape of a witch's hat hanging from an iron bracket. "Morgana's Millinery."

"If you're going to come in you'd better get a wriggle on, my little loves, I'm shutting up shop for Witching Hour in a minute!"

The girls looked around them and, sure enough, in neighbouring stores witches were busy locking shop doors and windows with enormous keys, then clip-clopping away over the cobbles and into the numerous coffee shops and bistros just springing into life for the evening.

"I thought Witching Hour began at midnight," Pru whispered to her friends.

"I guess anything goes in Raven Heights," Veronica replied.

Once inside, the three witches gasped as they looked around the boutique. Seemingly tiny from the outside, the shop had rows of shelves that rose up and up and up… further than the girls could see, with beautiful witches' hats in every shape and style imaginable, neatly displayed on them.

"We're looking for a rain hat," Veronica finally managed to blurt out, "you know, the one all…"

"… all the witches are wearing," interrupted Morgana. "I know, I know… I really should move them down to the bottom level. I've been up and down the entire height of this shop all week!"

The round-faced shopkeeper wearily lifted one short leg over her broomstick and rose up and up to the highest shelves of her boutique before returning to the shop floor with a thud.

"Oof! Came in a bit low that time," she chuckled, blinking and rearranging her half-moon spectacles into their correct position.

She placed three teetering hatboxes on the counter.

"I'm guessing you three young 'uns are off to the Black Rainbow Café for a Dead Bat Milkshake or something similar. That's where all the witches who buy these hats seem to hang out."

"Erm, yes… we are," Veronica said, winking animatedly at her friends. "I don't suppose you could point us in the right direction?"

"Bottom of Sad Rat Hill, opposite the Old Graveyard."

"Where else?" Pru muttered, rolling her eyes.

"That will be two galaxy notes, sixty moon coins, seven Jupiter pennies and 74 stars, please," the shopkeeper sighed, clearly in need of a hot cup of pumpkin tea.

Veronica quickly pulled her purse out of her hand-cauldron and handed Morgana three galaxy notes.

"Keep the change!" she called as the three witches skipped out of the shop.

Once they were outside, Veronica pulled her two friends in close.

"We need to go to the Black Rainbow Café and look for clues. Double-Bubble must have wanted us to try there."

"Well, let's go then," Figgy said, excitedly

arranging her new rain hat on her head and
setting it to "fine mist".

The walk down to the bottom of Sad Rat Hill
saw the last of the sun disappear and a wispy
fog begin to swirl about the witches' boots.

A group of very trendy-looking witches,
all wearing rain hats, were gathered outside

the Black Rainbow Café. Veronica, Figgy and Pru, rather awkwardly wearing their own new rain hats, made their way through the crowd and into the café with its stylish blue lighting and purple velvet furnishings. They even received approving nods from a couple of fellow rain hat-wearers. At the front was a stage where a witch was singing softly and mournfully into a microphone, her sequined dress shimmering magically under the blue lights.

"This place is beyond awesome," Figgy said, her voice barely audible it was so squeaky.

"I've never been anywhere so cool in my whole witching life," Veronica agreed, turning around in circles to take it all in – only to stumble over backwards onto Pru.

"Can we at least pretend to be cool?" said her friend scornfully.

"Okay, sorry. Let's go and get a warm drink, my rain hat is making me shiver," Veronica said, secretly wanting to take it off but not wanting to admit she wasn't cool enough to wear it.

The menu board behind the counter was even more confusing than the drinks list at the Belfry Bistro.

"I just want a hot chocolate with pumpkin spice," whimpered Figgy, her face shiny and wet from her rain hat.

"Good evening, Witchsters," said the waiter, whose rain hat was having its own full-blown thunderstorm. "What's it to be?"

Veronica frantically scanned the board for anything with the word chocolate in the title and ordered three of them.

"Good choice," he said, giving them an approving wink and placing three open-topped dragon's eggs on the counter.

The friends stared, jaws dropping as their drinks began to bubble. Three tiny baby dragon heads popped out of the chocolatey liquid and three miniature scaly dragon hands waved at them.

"Has your hot chocolate got a baby dragon in it too?" Figgy whispered in a slightly terrified tone.

"Yes," Veronica replied weakly, watching the baby dragon settle down comfortably into her drink as if it were having a warm bath before a sudden flurry of bubbles erupted from the depths. "And it's just farted in my hot chocolate."

Pru bravely took a sip of her drink, desperately trying to keep up the pretence of being cool.

"I think mine has done something in my drink too," she said, nose to nose with the baby dragon.

"Anyone else need the loo?" Veronica asked hopefully.

Before you could say "pumpkin puff" all three girls were hiding in the toilets, rain hats off and glad to be away from all the scary coolness in the café.

"Did either of you see any crows out there?" Veronica asked, dabbing her face dry with a paper towel.

"Every witch I could see had a crow as a familiar," Pru said in an exasperated tone. "It seems like Double-Bubble's shoulder crow craze has really taken off. There are no clues here. We're never going to find them."

"Wait, what's that?" said Figgy, wiping one finger over the mirror and sniffing the shiny pink gloop she had removed.

"Lip-gloss!" Veronica replied, looking closely at the fuchsia-toned slime. "And there's only one witch I know who wears that shade."

"Belinda Bullfrog! She's been here," Pru declared triumphantly.

"And look," Figgy continued, "there's more over here…"

The three witches followed the trail of gloss to the open window of the toilets.

"Bingo!" Veronica exclaimed, picking a black feather out of the smear of gloss on the window frame. "And it looks like she may have had some feathery friends with her!"

Veronica climbed out of the window and held up her hand to help her friends through too.

"I don't know where this glossy trail leads, but I just know Double-Bubble will be at the end of it," she said.

So with the moon high in the sky, the three friends set off through the cobbled streets to find Witch City's most famous girl band before Belinda Bullfrog ruined everything for good.

Chapter Six
The House of Crows

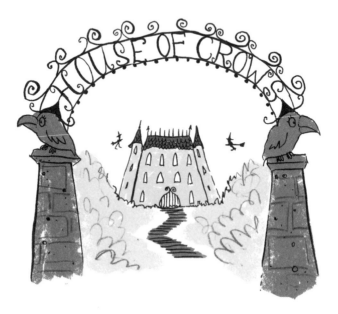

The three witches could hear the Belfry
clock chime seven o'clock as they arrived
at the gates of a tall, grimy stone building.
Behind the gates was a grand sweep of steps
peppered with groups of witches, huddling
together in the evening chill.

"What is this place?" Figgy asked in a quivering voice.

"I'm not sure, but it looks like a very exclusive apartment block," replied Veronica as she read the words 'House Of Crows' in intricate curving ironwork above the gates.

Sure enough, there were rows of very shiny, expensive-looking broomsticks gleaming in their parking places in the building's broom park.

"Look up there," Pru said, pointing to the turrets high on the building.

Circling in the sky were at least a dozen or so witches, flying around and around the penthouse apartment, seemingly trying to spy in through the windows.

Veronica approached a group sitting on the steps, their faces wet with tears.

"Excuse me," she said. "I'm sorry to disturb you, but can you tell me what's going on here?"

"Rumour has it that the penthouse is where Double-Bubble live… well, lived, before they were…" the witch took a deep breath and wailed "… kidnapped!"

Her witchy friends comforted her as she began sobbing hysterically.

Veronica turned to her friends.

"Double-Bubble said something interesting to me when I interviewed them earlier. They said that they always tell the press the opposite of what is true. So if rumour has it that Double-Bubble live on the top floor…"

"Then they live in the…" Figgy interjected.

"… basement," Pru said with uncharacteristic enthusiasm.

As they crept around to the back of the dark
building they found an open window and
climbed inside.

"This must be Jo and Kit's home, just look
at it!"

There were framed Double-Bubble gold discs
hanging on the walls and guitars leaning up

against the black damask wallpaper. A grand
piano stood in the corner with photographs of
the girls arranged on top in ornate frames. A
tall vase containing deep purple lilies wafted
a sweet aroma through the apartment, which
was dimly lit by candles flickering in a grand,
smoked-glass chandelier above their heads.
In the dim light, Veronica could just
make out something in the corner of
the room, hiding behind the piano.
It was tall and dark and draped in

deep plum-coloured silk. As she edged closer
to it she could hear a faint noise, which
grew louder the nearer she drew to the
shadowy object.

"SQUAWK SQUAWK SQUAAAAWK!"

Veronica jumped backwards in fright
and landed on top of Figgy, sending
them both into a crumpled pile
of pointy boots and black lace.
Pru strode over to the dark,
squawking object and pulled
back the plum silk cover.

The GLOOMIES

"It's Double-Bubble!" Figgy cried, sliding her glasses back on to her nose.

"Come on," Veronica said sharply as she rose to her feet. "Let's get you out of that cage!"

"Not so fast, darlings," came a smug voice from the other end of the apartment as Belinda Bullfrog appeared out of the darkness.

She had just put a fresh coat of sticky lip-gloss on her pursed lips and was still holding the pink wand.

"You've saved me the trouble of getting my new hair-do all wet by coming to me. Now I don't have to traipse across town, looking for you, and get my Mushroomo Batnik heels all muddy. This season's, don't you know?" And Belinda tilted her head so she could admire her very expensive designer shoes.

"Nice," Veronica retorted sarcastically, "but we're not staying. We've come to rescue Double-Bubble."

"Oh, have you?" Belinda laughed, a fake sound like a frog coughing up a fly. "I don't think so, darlings."

She looked at the lip-gloss wand she was holding, pouted, and while muttering a few magic words, pointed it at Veronica, Figgy and Pru. An arc of pink slime hit each of them straight in the face before Belinda popped the lid back on her gloss wand and folded her arms, smiling.

"Hah! Is that the best you've got?" Pru cried, feistily pulling her own wand out of her hand-cauldron, getting ready to give Belinda a taste of her own medicine.

"Silly witch," Belinda sneered. "Just you wait a minute."

Pru looked at Veronica and Figgy who were wiping pink slime off their faces before… poof! Pru disappeared and a shiny black crow appeared in her place. Then: **poof… poof…** two more crows replaced Veronica and Figgy.

Belinda laughed manically, exposing her lip-gloss-smeared teeth. She caught the three new crows and placed them in the cage with Double-Bubble.

"Now that I have you all safely locked away for eternity, darlings, I can tell you why you've ended up behind bars."

Belinda paced back and forth in front of the
cage, brandishing her lip-gloss wand in one
spray-tanned hand.

"Loose lips sink ships," she hissed. "I heard you bragging in the Cauldron Café this morning – you were so full of yourself, Veronica, boasting about your 'big exclusive interview'. What a shame that poor Figgy and Pru and Double-Bubble had to get caught up in your megalomania too. Now they'll be forced to live in a dark cage alongside you for ever."

Veronica squawked frantically at her cruel nemesis.

"Silly bird, be quiet," seethed Belinda. "I mean, why would such an incredible band as Double-Bubble want to do an interview with your silly little magazine when they could do one with *Nosy Toad* instead?

This time Double-Bubble squawked wildly, their little black eyes beady and cross-looking.

"So I followed you all on your journey to your 'big scoop', then when you had finished your interview, I approached Double-Bubble myself and offered them a deal that would far surpass anything you could ever offer."

A tear rolled down Figgy's black, feathery cheek and dripped off the end of her beak.

"But silly Double-Bubble turned down my generosity. So there was no other option but to teach them a lesson. Nobody ever says no to Belinda Bullfrog."

The five crows huddled together in their cage.

"So," Belinda continued, "you have a choice: give me that exclusive interview for my magazine or stay crows for ever. It's up to you, darlings."

Belinda stared at them and waited for a response.

All five crows shook their heads.

"No? Really? Silly birdies. Well, it's no matter to me, I've got a hundred more bands that are far more popular than Double-Bubble just dying to be featured in *Nosy Toad*. Enjoy your feathered future!"

And in the puff of pink smoke that only a witch as vain as Belinda would muster, she disappeared.

Chapter Seven
The Great Escape

"Now what?" Figgy chirped, wondering why everyone else's beak seemed to be shinier than hers.

"I'll think of something," croaked Veronica, still trying to get used to her own rather weird beaky face.

She looked over to Jo and Kit who were
snuggled together, their wings around
each other.

"I'm so sorry," Veronica cawed, "I feel like
it's my fault you're in this feathery fix."

"No, it's not your fault at all," chirped Jo.
"Belinda Bullfrog and her horrid magazine
have always been bad news. We know
you'll be able to figure out a way for us all
to escape. You're famous for all your bright
ideas at *Twitch*."

Veronica tried to smile and discovered that
crows can't. She thought hard for a moment.

"Okay, let's all swing this cage far enough
so I can reach into my hand-cauldron.
Then we can text for help."

 The five crows lurched backwards and forwards until the birdcage was swinging far enough for Veronica to stick out her beak and grab the handle of her hand-cauldron.

Pru poked her own beak through the bars and pulled out Veronica's phone, frantically pecking at the screen but to no avail.

"It's pointless – my beak's too hard and shiny. It keeps slipping off the touchscreen."

"Hang on." Figgy stuck her beak through the bars of the cage and into the bag, prising out a hair clip. "Let's try this."

Figgy wiggled the tiny clip around in the birdcage lock until the door sprang open and the five birds hopped out and onto the grand piano.

"Fantastic work," squawked Jo.

"We knew you'd get us out of this mess," croaked Kit.

87

'We're not out of the woods yet," Veronica warned, looking at her wings. "We're still crows and the only way to undo the spell and return to our witchy selves is to get our hands on Belinda's lip-gloss wand."

"But even if we do, how are we going to say the necessary words? We can't talk, only understand each other's squawks!" Pru was getting desperate now.

Veronica looked over to Double-Bubble's desk where their computer was still lit up.

"I've just thought of the most perfect plan ever. Let's do this!"

Chapter Eight
The Tables Are Turned

To: belindabullfrog@nosytoad.com

From: joandkit@double-bubble.com

Subject: Change of Heart...

Dear Belinda,

First, we must admit we managed to peck our way out of the cage, but never fear – we have locked up Veronica and her useless sidekicks so they can never get out.

We don't know what we were thinking of when we turned down your kind offer of an exclusive feature with the utterly fabulous *Nosy Toad* magazine. We'd love to do it and forget all about *Twitch* magazine. We want a big-time celeb mag like yours to cover us.

Could we fly over and meet you at the Grand Witch Arena where our next big gig, Witchfest, is being held? Maybe if you were to turn us back into ourselves you could get your team to take some exclusive photos of our warm-up and rehearsals.

We hope to hear from you soon.

Warmest and most sincere wishes,
Jo & Kit.

"Done!" Jo squawked as she finished tapping out on her computer the last words of the email that Veronica had just dictated. "My beak hurts now. I don't think they were designed for pecking emails!"

"Let's wait and see if we get a reply," Veronica crowed hopefully.

The five birds waited eagerly, Jo pressing 'refresh' every few seconds. Then it came…

ping!

From: belindabullfrog@nosytoad.com

To: joandkit@double-bubble.com

Subject: Change of Heart...

Dear darlings,

I knew you'd come round. See you there in ten. B.x

"She fell for it!" Figgy squawked with glee.

The five crows picked up their hand-cauldrons in their claws and flapped their way north-west over to the huge arena in the Crone's Corner area of the city.

They passed over the Black Newt river, sparkling under the city lights, swooping down over and under its bridges.

"Wow! Flying with wings is way better than flying on a broomstick," cawed Figgy as she twisted and turned in the night sky.

"I'm feeling a bit sick," Pru squawked, trying to fly in a straight line and not spill anything out of her hand-cauldron into the river below.

"There it is," Double-Bubble chirped in unison. "It's the Grand Witch Arena."

"Let's get inside before Belinda arrives!" Veronica was concerned that her plan would be ruined if their rival got there first.

As soon as the five crows swooped down into the open-air arena they flew around, switching on all the lights and cameras and the special effects that the stage team had set up ready for the concert.

"Here she comes," whispered Veronica. "Everyone, take your places!"

Figgy pulled a lever beside the grand stage and two holographic figures appeared in front of their eyes.

"Wow!" whispered Jo to
her sister.
"I never saw it from this angle before
as we're always on stage. They look so real!
Just like we're standing there."

A door opened at the back of the arena
and in walked Belinda Bullfrog.

"I knew it was too good to be true – of course
you were tricking me!" she hissed. "How did
you turn yourselves back into witches?"

The holograms carried on singing and
playing guitar on stage while the real Double-
Bubble stood watching in feathery form.

"I'll show you who's the boss witch
around here!" howled Belinda,
pulling out her lip-gloss
wand and pointing it
towards the stage.
"NOW!" squawked

97

Veronica, as Pru glided down with a voice recorder in her claws just as Belinda was muttering her magic words. And as the arc of pink slime-beam headed its way towards the stage, Figgy jumped out holding a mirror and directed it right back at Belinda.

Within a moment she was turned into a scraggly black crow, with a big beak and bow legs.

Veronica hopped over and grabbed the lip-gloss wand in her beak. While Pru pressed 'play' on the voice recorder and the magic transformation words were said aloud, Veronica pointed the wand at herself and her friends.

"Oh, thank my stars," Pru said, straightening her witch's hat into its correct position on her head. "It feels so good to have my arms and legs back!"

"I miss being a bird," Figgy said, rubbing the place where her beak used to be.

"Awesome!" Double-Bubble declared. "We were beginning to worry that we were going to have to cancel the Witchfest concert here at the arena and let all our fans down!"

"Teamwork! We couldn't have done it without you, Double-Bubble. Now, who fancies a dark hot chocolate?"

"ME!" everyone shouted at once.

"And let's not forget our new familiar," said Pru, picking Belinda up off the floor and fastening a lead around her neck.

"SQUAWK!" said Belinda.

"Oh, be quiet, you silly birdie!" Veronica told her as the new friends left to find a cosy place for a warming drink.

Chapter Nine

Pop, Pizza and PJs

Come on, witches,

don't be shy, Get on your

brooms and fly sky-high!

Double-Bubble's tuneful voices rang out over

the stadium full of witches, all dancing and
singing along.

Figgy was backstage, watching from the
wings, admiring the funky outfits she'd chosen
for the band to wear.

Pru was nearer the front of the stage, down
on one knee taking photographs of the
band and the cheering crowd.

"The atmosphere is electric," said Veronica
as she sidled up to Figgy, boogying along to

the beat. "I can't wait for the fashion shoot tomorrow, and then we'll have everything we need to run this feature in the next issue."

"Look at these shots," Pru said as she rushed over to her friends. "This is going to be the best issue of *Twitch* yet, I just know it."

"Thank you, Witch City, you've been awesome!" Double-Bubble hollered out to the crowd before running off stage towards Veronica, Figgy and Pru.

"You were incredible," Veronica told them, helping the sisters unstrap their guitars while Figgy handed them each a bottle of witch water.

"Thanks, girls. We're heading straight back to our apartment now for pizza. Would you like to join us?"

"Oh, yes, we'd love to," Veronica said as Figgy and Pru nodded excitedly.

Outside, a limo-broom was waiting and the five witches hopped on.

"Where to?" asked the driver.

"House of Crows," chirped Jo.

"Raven Heights," added Kit.

"Very good." The driver nodded, before sweeping the limo-broom in a wide semi-circle and then high up into the sky. Before long they swooped down around the back of the House of Crows. Double-Bubble pulled their lacy veils over their faces.

"You never know who's watching!" said Jo.

"You can say that again," said Veronica,

casting a sideways glance at Belinda, who squawked indignantly before Pru gave her lead a gentle yank.

The five witches entered Double-Bubble's apartment. Jo lit the chandelier and Kit disappeared into her bedroom before emerging a second later.

"Five pairs of cosy PJs!" she laughed. "Who wants to watch a film and eat pizza in true Double-Bubble style?"

"When we're not performing, we do this almost every night," Jo told them.

"But I thought you'd be out at all the trendy coffee shops and things here in Raven Heights!" said Figgy, astonished that the biggest girl band ever were so totally normal.

"Oh, we do occasionally. We like to go out, but we're at our happiest here at home with some tasty pizza and a good film."

"Look, the new season of *Which Witch Wins?* starts in ten minutes," Kit said, scrolling through the TV channels.

With everyone snuggled up in their pyjamas and the fire crackling away, the girls tucked into their pizza.

"I've just had the best thought ever," Pru said, suddenly sitting up and grabbing her camera. "Instead of having the photo shoot at the location I found, why don't we just do it here?"

"That's such a fabulous idea!" Veronica said eagerly. "It will really connect you with our readers and show how similar you are to them! Just normal girls relaxing at home in their PJs!"

"Genius!" Double-Bubble replied together.

"And what about Belinda Bullfrog?" Figgy queried, slipping the latest issue of *Twitch* magazine through the bars of the birdcage. "I'm sure she wouldn't want to be left out of the fun."

So the girls spent the evening dressing up in silly hats and oversized sunglasses, pulling funny faces as Pru snapped away with her camera.

Oh, and if you're wondering what happened to Belinda Bullfrog, I'm sure she was turned back into her true, mean self

… eventually.

WACKY BEE

Wacky Bee is a very small company but that doesn't mean that our ideas are small. Far from it! We have big ideas for our books. And because we're small and independent, it means that we can put those big ideas into action in exactly the way that we want… and have a lot of fun while we're at it. All Wacky Bee books have pictures. We love pictures!

Find out more about Wacky Bee at www.wackybeebooks.com

Other middle grade books by Wacky Bee:

Dougal Daley:
It's Not My Fault!
by Jackie Marchant,
ill. Loretta Schauer
978-0-9956972-2-5

Dougal Daley:
Where's My Tarantula?
by Jackie Marchant,
ill. Loretta Schauer
978-0-9956972-5-6

Dougal Daley:
I'm Phenomenal!
by Jackie Marchant,
ill. Loretta Schauer
978-0-9956972-6-3

Double Felix
by Sally Harris,
ill. Maria Serrano
978-1-9999033-0-5

Elise and the
Second-hand Dog
by Bjarne Reuter,
ill. Kirsten Raagaard
978-0-9956972-8-7